Well Done

An Ivy and Mack story

Written by Rebecca Colby
Illustrated by Gustavo Mazali
with Szépvölgyi Eszter

Collins

What's in this story?
Listen and say

Before reading 3

Ivy says, "I LOVE Sports Day!"

Mack says, "Croc loves Sports Day, too. And Mom and Dad!"

Mack says, "Look, Croc! Ivy is throwing the ball."

Mack is clapping. Mom and Dad are clapping.

Mack says, "Well done, Ivy! You're great!"

Mack and Croc are running.
Ivy says, "Run, Mack, run!"

His family are clapping.
Ivy says, "Hooray for Mack!"

Mack says, "Ivy is jumping. Wow! That is VERY good!"

Her family are clapping again.
Mack says, "Ivy is great!"

Ivy asks, "Where are Mack and Croc? Are they hopping?"

Ivy says, "Hop, Mack, hop!"

It's the egg and spoon race. Ivy is walking with her egg and spoon. Mack says, "Go, Ivy, go!"

Oh no! The egg ...

… FALLS!

Mack says, "Get the egg! Get the egg! Don't stop!"

Ivy looks at the children.
Ivy says, "Oh no!"

Mack says, "You LOVE Sports Day. Please finish, Ivy!"

Ivy listens to Mack. She gets the egg.

Ivy says, "You're right, Mack. I love Sports Day!"

Picture dictionary

Listen and repeat

clapping

hopping

jumping

running

throwing

walking

After reading

1 Look and order the story

2 Listen and say

Collins

Published by Collins
An imprint of HarperCollins*Publishers*
Westerhill Road
Bishopbriggs
Glasgow
G64 2QT

HarperCollins*Publishers*
1st Floor, Watermarque Building
Ringsend Road
Dublin 4
Ireland

William Collins' dream of knowledge for all began with the publication of his first book in 1819.

A self-educated mill worker, he not only enriched millions of lives, but also founded a flourishing publishing house. Today, staying true to this spirit, Collins books are packed with inspiration, innovation, and practical expertise. They place you at the center of a world of possibility and give you exactly what you need to explore it.

© HarperCollins*Publishers* Limited 2021

10 9 8 7 6 5 4 3 2 1

ISBN 978-0-00-848847-5

Collins® and COBUILD® are registered trademarks of HarperCollins*Publishers* Limited

www.collins.co.uk/elt

All rights reserved. No part of this publication may be reproduced, stored in a retrieval system, or transmitted in any form by any means, electronic, mechanical, photocopying, recording or otherwise, without the prior written permission of the Publisher or a license permitting restricted copying in the United Kingdom issued by the Copyright Licensing Agency Ltd, 5th Floor, Shackleton House, 4 Battle Bridge Lane, London SE1 2HX.

British Library Cataloguing in Publication Data

A catalogue record for this publication is available from the British Library.

All rights reserved. No part of this book may be reproduced, stored in a retrieval system, or transmitted in any form or by any means, electronic, mechanical, photocopying, recording or otherwise, without the prior permission in writing of the Publisher. This book is sold subject to the conditions that it shall not, by way of trade or otherwise, be lent, re-sold, hired out or otherwise circulated without the Publisher's prior consent in any form of binding or cover other than that in which it is published and without a similar condition including this condition being imposed on the subsequent purchaser.

Author: Rebecca Colby
Lead Illustrator: Gustavo Mazali (Beehive)
Copy Artist: Szépvölgyi Eszter (Beehive)
Series editor: Rebecca Adlard
Publishing manager: Lisa Todd
Product managers: Jennifer Hall and Caroline Green
In-house editor: Alma Puts Keren
Project manager: Emily Hooton
Editors: Deborah Friedland and Samantha Lacey
Proofreaders: Natalie Murray and Michael Lamb
Cover designer: Kevin Robbins
Typesetter: 2Hoots Publishing Services Ltd
Audio produced by White House Sound Ltd
Reading guide author: Julie Penn
Production controller: Rachel Weaver
Printed and bound by: Pureprint Group, UK

MIX
Paper from
responsible sources
FSC™ C007454
www.fsc.org

This book is produced from independently certified FSC™ paper to ensure responsible forest management.

For more information visit: **www.harpercollins.co.uk/green**

Download the audio for this book and a reading guide for parents and teachers at www.collins.co.uk/peapoddownloads